...And a Partridge in a Pear Tree

*A Unique and Humorous Parody of
"The Twelve Days of Christmas"*

Dick Foster

And a Partridge in a Pear Tree
Copyright © 2023 By Richard B. Foster
All rights reserved.

No part of this publication may be reproduced or transmitted in any form through electronic or mechanical means, including photocopying or otherwise, without permission in writing from the author.

This is a work of fiction. Names, characters, places, and incidents are the product of the author's imagination and are used fictitiously. Any resemblance to actual persons, living or dead, events, or locales is entirely coincidental.

For *Judy*

Acknowledgments

Thanks to Jeanne Moffitt for her help with proofreading and suggestions.

Thanks to all those who offered help and suggestions for this manuscript.

I am grateful for all the thoughtful suggestions and recommendations, but I printed the manuscript anyway.

"...but he that is of a merry heart
hath a continual feast."

Proverbs 15:15b

Table of Contents

Introduction 1

The Beginning 7

The First Day 10

The Second Day 14

The Third Day 18

The Fourth Day 22

The Fifth Day 28

The Sixth Day 34

The Seventh Day 39

The Eighth Day 47

The Ninth Day 56

The Tenth Day 63

The Eleventh Day 69

The Twelfth Day 75

Epilogue 82

Gift Inventory (in order of delivery) 85

Comments About the Book 87

A Gift for You 90

About the Author 92

Introduction

The popular song, "The Twelve Days of Christmas" was written in England many years ago by Frederic Austin. It describes the gifts given to a person's girlfriend over twelve days, with each day represented by a verse in the song.

It is a cumulative type of song in which each gift described in a verse is carried forward to the next verse. Each verse tells of a new gift received on that particular day, followed by all the previous gifts. Each of these gifts was given by the recipient's "True Love" during the twelve days after Christmas.

Many parodies have been written about "The Twelve Days of Christmas," perhaps more than any other Christmas song. The simple list of gifts encourages many imaginative gift substitutes. Some of these are very clever, indeed.

With that in mind, the song is the basis for this story. This is not a new version of the song with different types of gifts, but more of a literal interpretation of it. The story is built around the repetition of the gifts in each verse. In it, the recipient receives the number of gifts stated in each verse.

For example, on the second day, the gifts received are two turtledoves, a second partridge, and a second pear tree. At the end of the second day, the totals are two turtledoves, two partridges, and two pear trees. So, after some thought and calculations, the story was developed on that principle. Every day, a new gift is delivered, along with all the original gifts from the previous days.

Remember, no matter how frustrating and absurd the situation becomes, the plot is already set. Each gift in each verse must be sent, received, and dealt with, no matter how ridiculous it may seem. Here lies the fun and humor of the story. It should be read and enjoyed for that reason, and not taken seriously. After all, who in his right mind would send a lot of crazy gifts like this to his girlfriend? Or, who would continue to receive and put up with all these nutty gifts without trying to put a stop to it? In addition to that, the expense would be overwhelming!

Now, please don't judge the recipient too harshly. She only receives and responds to the gifts because the song says they were sent. In a way, she has no choice in the matter.

Before venturing into the story, I have listed each verse below to familiarize you with the song. Read the verses, and you will see how the story develops.

On the first day of Christmas,
My true love sent to me
a partridge in a pear tree.

On the second day of Christmas,
My true love sent to me
Two turtledoves,
And a partridge in a pear tree.

On the third day of Christmas,
My true love sent to me:
Three French hens,
Two turtledoves,
And a partridge in a pear tree.

On the fourth day of Christmas,
My true love sent to me:
Four calling birds,
Three French hens,
Two turtledoves,
And a partridge in a pear tree.

On the fifth day of Christmas,
My true love sent to me:
Five golden rings,
Four calling birds,
Three French hens,
Two turtledoves,
And a partridge in a pear tree.

On the sixth day of Christmas,
My true love sent to me:
Six geese a-laying,
Five golden rings,
Four calling birds,
Three French hens,
Two turtledoves,
And a partridge in a pear tree.

On the seventh day of Christmas,
My true love sent to me:
Seven swans a-swimming,
Six geese a-laying,
Five golden rings,

Four calling birds,
Three French hens,
Two turtledoves,
And a partridge in a pear tree.

On the eighth day of Christmas,
My true love sent to me:
Eight maids a-milking,
Seven swans a-swimming,
Six geese a-laying,
Five golden rings,
Four calling birds,
Three French hens,
Two turtledoves,
And a partridge in a pear tree.

On the ninth day of Christmas,
My true love sent to me:
Nine ladies dancing,
Eight maids a-milking,
Seven swans a-swimming,
Six geese a-laying,
Five golden rings,
Four calling birds,
Three French hens,
Two turtledoves,
And a partridge in a pear tree.

On the tenth day of Christmas,
My true love sent to me:
Ten lords a-leaping,
Nine ladies dancing,
Eight maids a-milking,
Seven swans a-swimming,

Six geese a-laying,
Five golden rings,
Four calling birds,
Three French hens,
Two turtledoves,
And a partridge in a pear tree.

On the eleventh day of Christmas,
My true love sent to me:
Eleven pipers piping,
Ten lords a-leaping,
Nine ladies dancing,
Eight maids a-milking,
Seven swans a-swimming,
Six geese a-laying,
Five golden rings,
Four calling birds,
Three French hens,
Two turtledoves,
And a partridge in a pear tree.

On the twelfth day of Christmas,
My true love sent to me:
Twelve drummers drumming,
Eleven pipers piping,
Ten lords a-leaping,
Nine ladies dancing,
Eight maids a-milking,
Seven swans a-swimming,
Six geese a-laying,
Five golden rings,
Four calling birds,
Three French hens,

Two turtledoves,
And a partridge in a pear tree!

<->

Whew! That does make for a relatively long and tiresome song. At the end of the story, I have listed a summary of all the gifts received, including the final counts. I didn't try to list the gift amounts, since the monetary value constantly changes. And now, on with the show—or rather, the story!

The Beginning

We begin at the beginning (where else?) with our heroine (the victim) remembering those crazy days after Christmas. Her name is Bunny, and she is reminiscing about her experiences (nightmares) of the last twelve days. Fortunately, she remembered to record all the events as they happened in a journal that could be used for future reference. It should be noted that some of her journal's future references could also be of help to her attorneys if necessary.

To begin with, Bunny is a young lady trying to make a decent living as an executive office secretary, despite her "True Love" and all his so-called gifts. It seems like somebody is always trying to mess up a good thing.

She has a good job, makes an excellent wage, and tries to lead a quiet life. Of course, she's not married (yet) and is in her middle twenties. She could be quite "ripe" for marriage if her True Love would act more sensible and not keep sending her a bunch of ridiculous Christmas gifts. But where would this story be without all his gifts? Anyway, this all fits quite nicely with "The Twelve Days of Christmas" song dialogue.

Bunny resides at a large farmhouse (with a barn and a large backyard) in the suburbs, since it would be rather difficult to live through these experiences if she were located in an apartment building. Just the milking maids and cows would contribute to a very crowded situation! Also, I don't think the neighbors in an apartment building would appreciate all the people stomping around as well as the various animals producing all kinds of screeching and bird calls, in addition to all sorts of odors (and that's only from the birds).

I'm sure that cows would not be appreciated by the apartment superintendent, either. The rest of these gifts are crazy enough without a bunch of cows wandering around outside an apartment building mooing and fertilizing ... well, never mind.

Now that we have Bunny properly situated, we'll have her continue with the narration of each miserable day by reading from her journal and adding a few explanations (or exclamations) as she progresses.

I should also mention that all these days do not run consecutively. There was a holiday and a Sunday in there somewhere, so no deliveries were made on those days. Bunny and the birds were all able to rest up before the next onslaught occurred.

Now, Bunny, behave yourself. No angry (or nasty) words. Remember, this guy is supposed to be your True Love (or whatever). So, enough said. Bunny, it's all yours.

•••• Bunny now continues with the narrative ••••

'Twas the twelfth day after Christmas, and all through the house—WHAT A MESS! Birds, eggs, trees, unnamed smells, and other items were everywhere! All these had occurred because of my True Love (used to be) and his attentive *generosity* toward me. Generosity? All that was generosity? All those animals and their..."calling cards"? If I ever get my hands on that guy again, I'll...well, maybe I'd better explain what happened. I need to calm down anyway.

It all started the day after Christmas when the first gift arrived. Just let me read from my journal, in which I recorded each memorable nightmare as it occurred.

The First Day

I will never forget that day when the front doorbell rang at 9:00 a.m. I had just finished eating my breakfast and was preparing to leave for work. The caller was a deliveryman with a rather large package for me. I thanked him and dragged it into my house. Oh, how exciting! It was always thrilling to receive a package, especially at that time of the year. The card on the box said it was from my True Love.

I opened it with great anticipation and excitement. Inside the box was a small tree in a wooden pot. The information card said it was a pear tree. I'd never had one of those—especially *inside* my house. What a nice Christmas gift. Then I noticed there was a small cage inside the box that contained a live bird. I found out later that this little bird was a partridge. I wasn't familiar with this type of bird—parakeets and canaries, yes, but not a partridge.

Later, I looked up the information on the partridge and discovered it was a medium-sized game bird and a bit smaller than a pheasant. I should have checked if it was good eating or not. I found out later that it was. I wondered if it tasted like chicken since everything else was supposed to taste like that. The information said it tasted more like duck. Oh well, for a Sunday dinner, who cared...chicken, duck, or whatever.

Well, I decided I'd better get a larger cage for that bird

before he flew right out an open door. Humph! I should have opened every door and window in the house, so the little...well, never mind. Sunday dinner, you know. I put the tree and caged bird on my heated back porch and left for work.

<->

During my lunch break, I went out to a pet shop and spent $75 on a larger cage for that miserable little fowl! I should have bought a cat! But I digress.

When I arrived home from work that evening, I decided to put the bird and the tree inside the new $75 cage since it was large enough to hold both items. Because I thought both the bird and tree looked quite attractive inside the cage, I decided to move everything into my living room. That was my *first* big mistake!

As I picked up the pot with the tree and started carrying it to the new $75 cage, I tripped on a footstool and took a tumble, spilling dirt from the pot all over my nice, clean carpet. Oh no! Black dirt on a light blue carpet.

I scooped most of the dirt back into the pot, straightened the pear tree, and carefully moved it into the cage. I stood there looking at my nice light blue carpet with a small coating of black dirt on it. I then noticed that the tree in the pot had recently been watered. Oh, great! I wondered if the black dirt stain would ever come out of my carpet.

I soaked a rag with water and scrubbed the stain on the carpet as best I could. Mistake number *two!* Never try scrubbing black dirt out of a light-colored carpet with just a wet rag. The stain only got worse. Now I'd have to have the carpet cleaned, all because of a dumb tree with a bird—and a footstool that got in the way of my foot.

I took the bird out of its original cage and carefully placed (stuffed) him into the new $75 cage next to the pear tree without getting any more stains on my carpet. The bird behaved himself. He seemed to adapt to his new environment quite nicely. He must have thought, boy, you sure are clumsy, lady.

I decided I'd try to cover the carpet stain by moving the new $75 cage containing the pear tree and bird on top of it. It was a perfect fit! The carpet cleaning could wait for a while.

<->

Later, as I was sitting on my sofa, I reflected on how thoughtful my True Love was in sending me this gift for Christmas. Thoughtful? A bird in a tree? I wondered *what* he was thinking. This *thoughtful* gift cost me $75 for a new birdcage. Oh, had I mentioned that before?

<->

I ate my supper while watching the bird in his cage and imagined what a partridge would taste like for Sunday dinner. The bird must have sensed something hostile from me because he moved toward the back of the cage and hid behind the tree.

After dinner, I read a magazine, then said goodnight to the occupants of the new $75 cage, and started upstairs to bed. Partway up the stairs, I suddenly realized I had just said goodnight to a bird *and* a pear tree. I thought I might be going a little crazy, but this was only the first day of my nightmares.

The Second Day

The following day, as I was eating my breakfast, the doorbell rang precisely at 9:00 a.m. It was the same pet store deliveryman from the day before with another package. Again, it was from my True Love. I was excited to see another gift from him.

This time the package contained a cage with two birds. More birds? The card that came with the package identified these birds as turtledoves. What beautiful sounds they made. My heart was singing along with them as I thought of my True Love's thoughtfulness. If I'd only known the true outcome of all this, my heart would have been singing a different tune toward him.

A couple of minutes later, the doorbell rang again. It was the same pet shop deliveryman. I guess he hadn't left yet. He had another package for me, which was also from my True Love. I thought I detected a chuckle from him as he walked back to his truck. Nevertheless, I quickly dragged the package inside, opened it, and found, to my surprise, *another* pear tree and *another* partridge!

I said to myself, "There must be some mistake—two trees with two birds. Hmmm. Maybe there's some hidden, secret meaning of love in this."

Anyway, after thinking it over, the only meaning that came to me was the need for another $75 cage for the new tree and new bird!

I dragged all the new boxes and items out onto my back porch. I figured I'd sort all this out when I got home later. I locked up the house and left for work.

<->

During my lunch break, I returned to the local pet store and spent another $75 on a new cage, much to the delight of the pet store owner. My investment was now $150 for two birdcages. Fortunately (or unfortunately), the birds that I'd received were free. So far, *their* "return on my investment" was precisely nothing. I wondered if I should open some windows in my house and allow them to really be free. No, not after my $150 investment. The birds would just have to put up with me—and me with them.

<->

Upon arriving home from work that evening, I took the new cage inside the house. I decided to move the *new* pear tree and partridge into the *new* $75 cage. This time I didn't trip over anything and spill any more dirt. My clumsiness had temporarily disappeared. I think the birds were a little disappointed in not witnessing another bumbling performance by me. Otherwise, everything went fine this time. I was getting better at this.

I decided to leave the older cage containing the other tree and bird just where it was in my living room. I still needed to cover up the dirt stain on my carpet. Because the two doves were already in a cage, I wouldn't need to buy another one.

I wondered if I had enough money left to buy my weekly groceries. Fortunately, I did and was able to go to the grocery store and restock my refrigerator that night. Oh, and I also bought some birdseed for my new *friends,* which my True Love had sent to me. At least it didn't cost as much as a $75 birdcage. The birds seemed to appreciate the birdseed, even though they didn't contribute anything to its cost.

<->

That evening as I ate my dinner, I once again stared at both partridges in their cages and watched their near panic-stricken reactions as they nervously moved toward the back of the cage and hid behind the tree. I was enjoying this. The new birds (doves) didn't seem to care at all. They were more interested in each other.

After finishing my dinner and cleaning up the kitchen, I fed the birds and watered the trees. At least I didn't *feed* the trees and *water* the birds. I still had my wits about me.

I then went back into the living room and sat down to watch TV. The noise from the TV programs seemed to pacify the birds a little as they just sat and watched it with me. The pear trees, however, didn't say anything. They just sat there. At least I didn't *hear* anything from them. I chuckled a little as I thought about that. I wasn't going crazy after all. At least, not yet.

After my evening's entertainment (?), I started towards the stairs to go up to my bedroom. I stopped and looked behind me and noticed the birds were quiet and not moving. The TV programs seemed to put them to sleep. Unfortunately, it was only temporary.

That night, I had trouble sleeping due to the occasional "bird calls" from the downstairs living room. I knew it wasn't the partridges because they hadn't uttered a sound since they had moved in...not so with the doves. They were making a lot of "cooing" noises and such. I figured I would eventually get used to it, and the birds would get used to me.

I then remembered that these gifts were from my True Love and that I should be more appreciative of him. I finally went to sleep thinking about his thoughtful, or rather thought-provoking, gifts. The birds finally settled down around 2 a.m.—kind of like some of the neighbors' late-night parties.

The Third Day

The next day I left for work early and missed any possible pet shop shipments. I thought these deliveries should have stopped by now since I already had enough birds and trees.

Things went well at my job that day, and I was able to get a little ahead of schedule, which was beneficial after the Christmas season. I was hoping that my True Love would stop by and see me personally, rather than through a bunch of birds and trees. Unfortunately, that was not to be.

<->

I returned home that evening only to find three more boxes on my front porch. The pet shop deliveryman had not forgotten me. I checked all the packages carefully and dragged them inside the house. I then moved all the new boxes to the back porch in case there were any new "surprises." After feeding all the current resident birds, I went out onto the back porch and began opening the new packages. Again, these were from my True Love.

With an excited (but skeptical) heart, I opened the first one, and to my amazement, there were three *new* birds.

According to the information card on their cage, these were called French hens. *French* hens? Why foreign birds? They certainly looked like normal chickens to me. I wondered if they clucked in French. I bet they tasted like regular chickens, though.

By now, I was beginning to wonder what kind of a "birdbrain" this True Love guy was. I set the new cage containing the French chickens to one side of my back porch and looked at the other boxes.

Cautiously, I started to open one. I gasped in surprise as I opened the package. There were two more birds— the turtle dove kind. By now, I was getting pretty good at recognizing these birds. I think I was becoming a bird expert since I had enough of them. I now had four doves, fortunately in two cages. Two doves were enough, but why four?

Anyway, I set them next to the other two doves, and they immediately began communicating like they hadn't seen each other for two years. They had probably been together in the same pet shop for that long!

I glanced at the remaining package with reluctance. "Hmmm, I wonder...same size, same shape," I said. I opened it. Yep, just as I thought. Another tree (the pear type) with another bird (the partridge type). What now? Had the pet shop made a mistake? Had the deliveryman made a mistake? No, they couldn't have. Who else would want a bunch of birds? I certainly did not, but my True Love thought I did.

What did I want with three more birds and trees? Would I need to go out and buy another $75 cage? Of course not! The pet store was making enough money off my True Love and me as it was.

I decided to carefully move the trees out of each of the cages and place them around my Living room. I would then stuff the new fowl in a cage with one of the others and forget about it. Forget about it? With all these birds clucking, cooing, and...I stopped and thought about my True Love. How thoughtful, how imaginative, how gracious, how...*weird*! Ten birds! I'd never even owned one bird, let alone ten! Well, if I was going to get any sleep that night, I'd have to leave the birds on the back porch and put some covers on those cages. Hopefully, that would prevent them from communicating with each other all night. I certainly didn't want any all-night "parties" going on in my house, even with a bunch of birds!

I rummaged around in my hall closet and looked for some covers to use. I moved a box to one side on the top shelf and was met with an avalanche of sheets, pillows, and numerous other items cascading all over me. After picking myself up off the floor, I looked around at the mess piled up around me. I didn't know I had all this stuff.

I finally found some sheets that looked like they would cover all the cages nicely. I then looked around at the rest of the stuff scattered on the floor. I was planning to rearrange those shelves in the closet anyway, but I wasn't expecting to do it this soon. Oh well, I decided there was no time like the present.

My rearrangement went as follows: (1) Open the closet doors, (2) Pick up all the items around me, and (3) Fling them into the closet while quickly closing the doors. There, that was all taken care of. I sure loved temporary rearrangements.

I then set about covering all the occupied cages. I then stopped and said, "Wait a minute, what am I thinking? Which cages are *unoccupied*?" I realized that if there were any, then some of the birds were loose and flying around my house. I checked again, found no empty cages, and decided *I* might be the one who was becoming unoccupied or was losing something! I guess I was getting tired of this bird menagerie and not thinking straight.

I piled the spare sheets in a corner on the porch (what was I anticipating?), said goodnight to all the birds, and began to enjoy the peace and silence. I climbed up the stairs to my bedroom and finally got some rest that night. So did the birds.

The Fourth Day

After breakfast the next morning, I uncovered the cages, fed the birds, watered the trees, and got ready for work. Again, I didn't get the two mixed up. I was getting good at this. I was beginning to feel like a gardener and a birdkeeper. Maybe I could get a job at a zoo?

Once again, I left for work early, thinking that I had missed the deliveryman. Nah, he wouldn't be delivering any more packages again. This incident of birds and trees had to be over. After all, nobody in their right mind would keep sending a bunch of birds to me, not even my True Love. Well, no one in their *right mind* anyway.

My workday proved uneventful until I returned home that evening. As I turned into my driveway, I suddenly stopped and stared at my front porch. It looked like a garage sale in the middle of July! There were packages all over the place.

"Oh no," I said, "not again!"

I shook my head in disgust and drove on into my garage. At least I remembered to raise the garage door first. This bird "business" was affecting my thinking!

I closed and locked the garage, and as I entered the house through the back porch, I was greeted with all kinds of birdcalls, along with some strong odors.

"Guess I'd better leave a window open tomorrow," I said to nobody in particular as I wrinkled up my nose and headed for the living room. "Whew! I'd better open some now!"

"Hello, birds!" I shouted, causing a moment's silence. I had moved all the cages and birds inside the house since it was getting rather cold, even for my heated back porch. As I made my way to the front of the house, the noise level reached its peak again. With a sigh, I opened the front porch door to retrieve all the packages that I was now accustomed to receiving.

"Yep," I said, looking over the boxes, "they're all here and accounted for." I found the one with the bird and tree, the one with the doves—who were already "cooing" at each other—and the box with the foreign birds. That's a total of six French chickens. At least they're an even number now.

As I finished opening the boxes containing all the regular birds, I began tearing open the new box. "Now, I wonder what this is?" I said to any of the birds that might be listening. I certainly didn't need any *more* birds. I had enough of them already.

Looking at the card on the box, I said, "Well, let's see. It's from my True Love, all right." I opened the box, and there was...now, what?

"What kind of birds are these?" I said aloud. "Hmmm, there are four of them, and what's the card say? 'Calling birds'...Calling birds? Why do I need some calling birds? I've got too many birds now! What's with this guy?"

I suddenly stopped and looked around at all the birds and their silence. They seemed to be staring at me as if to say, *Who are you talking to, lady? We're just a bunch of dumb birds who can't answer back.*

I was tempted (only tempted) to leave some of the birds and cages on the front porch with the windows open, but, cruelty to animals, you know.

After situating the four new birds in another corner of my living room (fortunately, there was a cage included), I stuffed the new partridge in with the other single one and moved the new arrivals in with some of their predecessors, trying to save cages in case I needed them in the future. I was thinking ahead.

<->

I had just sat down for my dinner thinking that everything was fine when I heard a tremendous ruckus in the living room! And it wasn't Santa's sleigh and reindeer falling off the roof.

"What in the world?" I exclaimed. "Was there a cat inside one of the boxes? Boy, wouldn't that be nice!"

I jumped up and hurried into the living room. As I entered the room, I noticed the commotion coming from one of the cages containing the foreign birds. There was a terrific fight being waged!

Now that's just what I needed, another world war. As I looked inside that cage, two, three...no, five birds were all trying to kill each other! Feathers were flying everywhere inside that cage. They were screeching at each other so loudly that the other birds had stopped singing, or whatever they were doing, to watch the action. I suspected that one or two of them might have been taking bets on the outcome.

I then discovered what was wrong. I had accidentally

stuffed two of the doves in the cage with the French chickens, and somebody must have disagreed with the seating arrangements for dinner! I was tempted to let them continue going at it until they all killed each other, but I decided I'd better not. Not a bad temptation, though.

I determined that I'd better intercede before I had to take care of a dead bird or two. I picked up the cage, opened its door, and dumped all the birds onto the floor.

The shock of a "referee" interfering with their argument must have been too much for them, because they immediately stopped fighting and began walking around in a daze. I assumed the other birds were paying off their bets, since it became quiet once again and they were no longer cheering for a winner but were just watching the proceedings.

I picked up each bird from the floor and stuffed it inside the cage with the other appropriate birds. Now the accommodations were correct for each species of bird. They all must have agreed since quietness now reigned throughout the living room. World War III was averted.

I went back to my dinner, mumbling under my breath about my True Love. This "bird business" was getting out of hand and had to stop! I scowled at some of the foreign chickens and thought about Sunday dinner. They must have sensed something from my look as they quietly moved toward the back of their cage. I think some of their toughness had disappeared, and they were learning how to behave.

<->

After dinner, I cleaned the kitchen, living room, and

both porches and began thinking about the future. I thought about staying home from work the next day to prevent the pet shop deliveryman from leaving any more birds. However, I decided my job and paycheck were more important. Besides, how else was I going to feed myself and these uninvited "boarders." I figured I'd better go to work regardless of the arrival of any more front porch boxes. Who knows, maybe this would be the last of them.

<->

Just before going up to bed, I took an inventory of what I had received from my "questionable" True Love during these last four days and arrived at the following totals:

4 **Pear trees** - All were in decorative wooden pots with rich, black dirt. I was hoping that these could be transplanted (outside, of course) and produce some delicious fruit.

4 **Partridges** - These birds were very quiet and were constantly following me with their eyes. Maybe they were afraid they were going to become Sunday dinner.

6 **Turtledoves** - Despite their constant "cooing", they were love birds.

6 **French hens** - Well, they might be beneficial as a special dinner.

4 **Calling birds** - Who were they constantly calling? Each other, I guess. I wouldn't be surprised if they had cell phones and were calling their bookies!

That was a total of 20 birds—**20** birds! I decided I'd better get some more birdseed.

The Fifth Day

I was running a little late this morning and was just eating my breakfast when the doorbell rang. I wondered who could be at my door at 8:30 in the morning. "It's too early for the man with my *daily* delivery of trees and birds." I chuckled as I walked toward the front door, almost afraid to open it.

I opened it anyway, and there stood a different man with a small package in his hand. At this early hour, I knew it had to be some kind of a special delivery. He confirmed that my name matched the one on the package, had me sign a receipt, and handed the package to me. He smiled, wished me a "Good day!" and left. Now what, I thought?

"Maybe it's a hummingbird," I said as I went back to finish my breakfast, taking the small package with me. I decided to open it and get it over with. Once again, the accompanying card indicated that it was from my True Love. Removing the wrapping paper revealed what looked like a jewelry box.

"Hmmm," I said. "That deliveryman's van did look like some sort of reinforced vehicle, now that I think about it." Some of the birds looked at me as if to say, *Who are you talking to, lady? We're still just a bunch of dumb birds sent here to make your life miserable.*

I excitedly opened the box to find...a GOLD ring! No, not one or two, but FIVE gold rings! They all looked like pure gold. I examined the inside of one of the rings. It was stamped with *24k!* It was **24-carat** gold!

"WOW!" I shouted, scaring all the birds into silence. I almost passed out as I stared in awe at the gleaming golden objects. I thought of my True Love and the sacrifice he must have made for these. Why, these rings had to be worth hundreds, maybe even thousands of dollars!

These were undoubtedly worth all the trouble I had been having with those birds. Maybe my True Love was feeling guilty for sending me all those birds, and this was his way of apologizing. Nah, I didn't think so.

Then I began to wonder about the cost of those very expensive rings. "Hmmm, I wonder where he got the money to pay for these?" I questioned. The birds looked at me again, probably wondering who I was talking to. "Well, it is kind of curious," I said to them, as they just stared back at me.

As I finished my breakfast with great excitement, I slipped one of the gold rings onto a finger on my *right* hand (I was beginning to have doubts about this guy).

I took the ring box containing the other four rings upstairs to my bedroom and hid it in the back of a dresser drawer. I realized that was probably the first place a thief would look for valuables, but I didn't have much choice for hiding places. I'd just have to take a chance that a thief might be dumber than me.

I also decided to buy a small safe during my lunch

hour. I felt better since I didn't have to buy anything for those birds again. I determined that this upcoming purchase was much more practical and useful.

I hastily finished getting ready for work and hurried downstairs. I said goodbye to the birds and happily started out the door for work. I noticed they merely looked at me like I was some kind of nut! Well, what did they know? At least I was a *happy* nut with five new gold rings!

<->

I positively enjoyed my day at work, making a few of my coworkers ponder what was wrong with me. Several privately questioned each other about my happy attitude, but they were unable to determine any apparent reason for it.

During my lunch hour, I went out and purchased a small safe at a fairly reasonable price. The salesman insisted on helping me load it into the trunk of my car because he thought it was too heavy for me to carry alone. I thought that was a very nice thing for him to do, but I wondered who was going to help me unload it and lug it into my house.

Fortunately, I didn't have too much trouble lifting my new purchase out of the trunk of my car when I got home. I only dropped it on my foot once during that operation. I managed to drag the safe into the house and up the stairs to my room. I only dropped it on my other foot twice while lugging it up the stairs.

After finally reaching my bedroom, I dragged it across the room and set it in a corner by my dresser. I covered it with some empty boxes, sheets, and pillows. I figured a thief wouldn't discover it right away—unless he was trying to steal empty boxes, sheets, and pillows. Of course, nowadays, you'd never know. There are a lot of nutty people around. My birds would affirm that.

Pulling open the dresser drawer, I confirmed that the jewelry box was still there, and breathed a sigh of relief. I removed it and placed it on top of my dresser. I opened it, admiring the gold rings my True Love had sent me. Oh, what a wonderful gift! I still wondered where he was able to obtain the money to purchase something as expensive as this.

I opened my brand-new safe and placed the box of rings inside of it. The safe looked kind of empty with just the jewelry box there, so I thought I'd better put some of my more important papers in there, too. Besides, it would cover up the ring box, giving it a little more added protection. I decided to take care of that right after my dinner.

My heart was so filled with joy that I didn't even hear the birds and their noises, let alone notice the strange odors. I suddenly remembered the birds in the living room and hurried downstairs. I went after the bird seed and dumped more than an ample portion into each cage, feeling very generous that evening. The birds looked at me as if to say, *What now?* I didn't care. I had five gold rings, probably worth thousands of dollars.

I then thought about the front porch and decided I'd better check it out, just in case. After sending the gold rings to me, I figured my True Love must be nearly out of money, and all those crazy gifts would finally end. How wrong I was!

I opened the front door, and there were the usual

packages! I was tempted to leave them outside to the elements but decided I didn't want the animal control people after me for showing cruelty toward animals.

"Cruelty toward animals? What about cruelty toward humans?" I said aloud. But, I decided I'd better take care of all these "foul" little fowls.

However, these birds are fowls, not land animals. Birds fly around and die all the time during the winter months, and...oh, never mind. I erased the thought from my mind and proceeded to drag each box to the back porch. I was getting this routine down to a science now. That was scary.

I then opened all the regular boxes Yep, I received the same things again: a partridge (that's five, now), two more doves (that's eight of those), three more foreign birds (that makes a total of nine), four "calling" birds (they're up to eight), and, oh yes, another pear tree (that's five of those). I made sure this time that I put no odd species of birds together in the same cage. After all, I sure didn't want another war to start in this house.

Well, at least I didn't have to buy any new cages—yet. But, tomorrow, I would have to do something drastic if any more of these creatures arrived. I knew I could only stuff so many of the same birds into one cage without causing problems among the "friendly" ones or those of identical species.

<->

After I ate my dinner, I cleaned the house a little and opened a few windows. These birds were coming on a little strong now. More air circulation was needed.

I also figured I would have to start moving any new

arrivals onto the back porch since I was running out of space inside the house. I was thinking ahead again. There was only so much room remaining inside my house for all these "freeloaders."

Finally, I covered all the cages, said goodnight to the birds, and went upstairs to bed. Thus ended the fifth day of these adventures.

The Sixth Day

Much to my surprise, the same jewelry deliveryman arrived early this morning with (gasp!) five *more* gold rings! He handed me the package containing the rings, had me sign the receipt, and left. He's such a nice man, I thought, especially since he keeps delivering me those rings. As I contemplated what to do with these expensive items, the pet store delivery van arrived.

"Oh no," I exclaimed, "not again! I don't have any more room or cages or...oh, well." I felt like running and hiding so I wouldn't have to answer the door, but he would just leave all the boxes on the front porch anyway. I relented and opened the door at his knock. This time there were four boxes plus a new one. He smiled, said hello and goodbye, and left very quickly. He sure was in a hurry this morning. Did he know something I didn't know? Uh-oh, I didn't like the look of this.

I checked over the regular boxes and then the new box. Now, what new gift was this "birdbrain" sending to me this time? I dragged all the boxes to the back porch, which had now become my "unloading" dock.

I opened the regular boxes and unloaded the now familiar birds. Very carefully, I moved some of the cages of creatures to various locations on the back porch, along with the new pear tree. The living room was becoming rather crowded, so the back porch had now become the new bird sanctuary.

With slight fear and trembling, I now turned to the new package. It looked about the same size as the other boxes, but I had a sinister feeling about it. I wanted to pick it up and throw it out the back porch door. Nevertheless, I took a deep breath and tore off the top cover.

<->

I was suddenly greeted with a *panic-stricken* "honking" noise. I jumped back and took a closer look inside the box. There were six (I counted them twice) full-grown geese! They were all packed tightly together inside the package and were trying to forcibly take possession of the area outside of the box—where I was!

As I moved my hand toward the edge of the box, one of those geese tried to nip it off! I raised my hand in a mock gesture to clobber the offending bird but was halted by more honking and displeasure from those birds. I could see that these waterfowl and I were NOT going to get along at all!

I immediately decided that these birds would not have the run of the house as they wanted to. However, I couldn't leave them outside in the cold (cruelty to animals, you know), so I decided to move them to the darkness of my basement, hoping they would sleep a lot. I figured if I couldn't sell them, each of these birds would soon decorate my dining room table as a special dinner I had planned for my True Love. That would certainly be a "fowl" dinner!

Dodging a couple of attacks by those geese, I quickly closed and temporarily sealed the top of the box. That seemed to stir them up more, but I knew I only needed a minute to move them over to the basement door. I hoped that would be enough.

I picked up the box of angry fowl and started to carry it through the living room to the basement. I decided to check out the basement first before I ventured across the living room with that box of angry creatures. I set the box down, then walked over and opened the basement door. "Ah, good. Nice and dark in the basement," I said. "That should be just right for those geese and hopefully keep them under control—and away from me!"

I returned, picked up the box of geese, and started for the now-opened basement door. Forgetting I had set a pear tree in the middle of the room, I ran headlong into it, knocking it over and losing my balance. While still hanging onto the box of geese, I tried desperately to regain my balance by twisting, turning, and throwing one leg into the air but only succeeded in falling flat on my...well, falling to the floor.

The box went flying across the room, dumping its contents of wild "honking" geese onto the floor. Without even waiting to see if *I* was all right, they scurried off for more interesting parts unknown inside my house, letting their presence be known with an occasional "honking" sound, which sounded more like a victory cry of "We finally escaped! The place is ours!"

Oh, great! Now I had six "foul" waterfowl roaming the house. I looked around at some of the other birds. It looked like they all were snickering, if not laughing hysterically. I think these birds were beginning to enjoy my antics and their "unwelcome" stay with me.

I walked over to the basement door, kicked it closed, and looked around dejectedly and painfully. With pain now arising in my foot from kicking the door, I angrily looked at the other birds in the living room, who had now all moved to the back of their cages, trying to hide from me. I picked up the box that had lately contained the six geese and heatedly tossed it across the room. As it hit the wall, something flew out and landed a few feet from me with a "plop."

"What now?" I said as I limped over and looked down at the now broken object, oozing its contents onto my beautiful (used to be) living room carpet. An egg!

"Oh no! Just what I *don't* need—pregnant geese!" I said in disgust. Besides me, my carpet was taking a beating. First, black dirt from a pear tree, and now an egg from a goose. All these gifts were starting to cause serious problems not only for my carpet but also for me.

I would soon discover that other "delicate objects" of this sort (eggs) were now being "deposited" in various areas around my house. And some of these objects would, unfortunately, be discovered by the bottom of my foot.

I began carrying a rag and a dustpan around with me to clean up any broken eggs I came in "contact" with. Anyway, I knew that at least *one* of the geese was a female. If most of them were pregnant mothers, I was certainly going to experience a population explosion of geese—another horrible nightmare! I began walking around with my head down, constantly looking ahead for any waiting "land mines."

I quietly and cautiously took another turn around the house, carefully watching for any of the missing geese. Unfortunately, my mission failed. They were all too clever—and well-hidden. I wondered if they were wearing radios to warn each other of my reconnoitering. It was probably better that I didn't find any of these reprobate geese, or someone (me) might have been killed! I decided I'd better find a weapon and start carrying it around the house for my protection.

<->

That evening after dinner, I made another quick trip to the pet shop to purchase more bird seed and another $75 cage, much to the delight of the pet store owner. I returned home, hoping to catch at least one goose at a time so I could begin my True Love's special dinner preparations. I had decided that *his* "goose" was going to be cooked!

I fed all the other birds and covered the cages for the night. I also opened a couple more windows to air out the place. After locking up and turning out the downstairs lights, I grabbed a broom (as a weapon) and cautiously ascended the stairs, watching and listening for a loose goose.

Once I was safely in my room, I carefully looked around there for any more *rogue* geese. Finding none, I locked myself in and went to bed.

The Seventh Day

My nerves were becoming frayed. I couldn't walk anywhere in my house without being attacked by a startled goose. Those monsters were lying in wait (when not laying eggs) to *ambush* me from every corner of the house. My home had become a refuge for birds! If I could ever get hold of my not-so True Love...well, that's a thought for another day.

Fortunately for him, he was out of town on business, as I soon discovered after 45 calls to his office. However, no one seemed to know what "business" he was out of town for. And, no one knew where he was. Hmmm.

I began to wonder what he had against me or what I had done wrong. I was also contemplating how *true* his love for me was when the doorbell rang. Oh yes, 8:30 a.m.—the "golden" spot of the day.

I received the new set of gold rings from the deliveryman and closed the door. Was that some special smile and a wink he gave to me? I made a mental note to double-check for another wink and a smile if he showed up again tomorrow. I certainly hoped he would—along with his gold rings, of course. I also decided to rent a safe deposit box at my bank and transfer some of those rings to it. I would rest more comfortably without having all those rings around the house. I also contemplated selling some of them for cash.

I was about to leave for work when the doorbell rang again. "Oh no," I said, "they're coming earlier now." Yep. Five boxes, all delivered and accounted for. That did it! I grabbed my hat and coat, slipped on my shoes, and started to race outside when I suddenly felt a cold, mushy, icky feeling inside my right shoe. The goose that belonged to that egg was going to be cooked if I could ever catch it!

I was determined to take action this time. I had to get rid of all these birds and stop any new "freeloaders" from arriving! Deciding I would be late for work or just not make it there that day, I stomped out the back door (egg and all), got into my car (after dumping the contents of my shoe on the grass), and headed straight for the downtown pet shop.

I arrived there and found, to my dismay, that it was closed. A sign on the door said something about being temporarily closed for the day to restock their inventory of various birds. If the place had been open, I could have easily restocked it for them. I was the one who had most of their stupid birds!

I shook my head and walked slowly back to my car, wondering what to do next. The acquisition of a cat crossed my mind, but I decided that wasn't a very good idea since I had spent most of my money on food for those miserable birds. That would certainly be a bad "return on my investment". Besides, the pet shop was closed, and I didn't want to merely pick up any old cat off the street, even if it might be free. No doubt the geese

40

would probably kill *any* cat I brought home anyway! Even an alley cat deserved a better chance than that. I got into my car and drove home.

As I turned into my driveway, I saw the array of boxes that I had left on the porch. Suddenly, panic gripped me! Like a football player, all I wanted to do was to scream and kick—boxes! After telling myself to calm down (I'd been talking to myself a lot lately—it was sure better than talking to those birds), I drove on out to my garage.

I parked my car, went around to the front of the house, and slowly climbed the porch steps. As I looked inside the porch, all I saw were boxes, boxes, and more boxes! I was getting tired of looking at those every day. Oh well, what could I do but empty them? I entered the porch, checked over the packages, and recognized all but one of them.

It looked like all the usual stuff—trees and birds. Wait...oh no, not more geese! I felt like dumping the contents of that box *outside* my house this time, but I was afraid those geese might attack some of the neighbors. I was already in enough trouble with the neighborhood, and I didn't want a war to break out between the neighbors and this army of geese! The neighbors might lose!

I could just see the news report: "An army of rogue geese terrorized a neighborhood! The National Guard was called in to restore order! The Geese refused to negotiate peace terms! War continues!"

No, I certainly couldn't allow those monsters to roam the neighborhood. I would just have to take care of them myself.

I carefully carried all the regular boxes (I was getting

stronger) into the house. By walking very carefully, I managed to step on only three goose eggs. I was getting better. Soon, I would become an expert at dodging the little things and be able to pursue the art of tiptoeing through the tulips— or rather, the goose eggs.

After all the boxes were inside, I carefully identified each one. Yes, that looked like the box that contained those lousy geese! I gently nudged it with my foot. Yep. There was that telltale "honking." Oh, brother, more pregnant geese. What possessed that birdbrain to send me so many birds?

Oops, I forgot to call him my True Love. Could something be happening to me? Hmmm, I wondered. Maybe I was going crazy! Nah. *He's* the one who was crazy!

After checking the glass-enclosed back porch, I determined that it was warm enough (and strong enough) to hold all the new arrivals, and I proceeded to move all the boxes out there. After successfully relocating everything (without tripping or spilling any), I opened each box and placed the new occupants in various places on the back porch. Thank goodness for old farmhouses and large porches.

I figured it wouldn't be too cold for any of those little...ah, birds. I decided to unpack the noisy geese last, which, by now, were honking their heads off! They were also so excited that they were jumping and banging around the inside of their box, making the box bounce around the porch floor! They acted like they couldn't wait to get out and attack someone—namely me! I would have to be very careful not to provoke any attacks by those hyperactive creatures. Provoke an attack? Those monsters were ready to attack anything or anybody at a moment's notice without any provocation!

I decided to move closer to the door of the house (for my safety and protection) before dumping over the box of geese. However, upon checking the door, I found that it was LOCKED! It had slammed shut as I was moving the boxes out to the back porch. I remembered that my house key was in my coat—which was inside the house!

Those "foul" flock of birds had done it to me again (with a little help from me)! As I pondered the situation, I realized that my only hope was to check to see if the front door was unlocked. If not, I would have to try crawling in through a window. Well, try to, anyway. That choice didn't excite me very much, since I wasn't very good at climbing things.

I considered leaving the back porch door open, hoping a neighbor's cat would come to investigate. No, I thought, I'd better not. I didn't want the cat killed by these hostile geese. After all, it was "six-to-one" in favor of the geese. The cat wouldn't stand a chance, not even with "one-to-one" odds!

I moved to the back porch door, quickly dumped over the box, pushed the door open, and dashed outside, slamming it behind me. Ha! Those geese never even knew I'd left. Score *one* for me!

I walked around to the front of the house. When I reached the front door, I discovered it was locked. Score *one* for the geese! Fortunately, I had left one of the front windows open to eliminate some of the obnoxious smells from inside the house and decided I'd have to climb up and crawl into the house that way.

During that maneuver, however, I realized I needed

43

to join a fitness club since I had a rather difficult time squeezing my "caboose" in through the window. I told myself that the window had just gotten smaller due to outside moisture or something like that. It must have been quite a sight for the neighbors to see. I thought I heard some hilarious laughter coming from down the street but decided it was probably just the wind.

Once inside again, I returned to the front porch to check out the new box that had been delivered that day. It seemed larger and heavier than the others. Well, maybe my "friend" had run out of birds to send. After all, he'd only sent me 62 of them! Why would I want any more?

I tore off the top of the box and...now what? Inside the box, I found a small fountain or pool filled with water and one, two, three...no, seven swans! Oh great! That was now 69 birds that "creep" had sent to me!

Oh well, I had always wanted a swimming pool for my house. However, I preferred one that was a little larger than four feet in diameter. I liked to swim, but in a much larger pool that would accommodate my, ah, expanding anatomy.

I looked around my living room, selected an open spot (of which there were few left), and dragged the box to that spot. I tore away the rest of the box and carefully removed its contents. At least there weren't any more eggs. I had "found" enough of them already. Or, I should say, my *feet* had found them.

I positioned the pool with the seven swans swimming around in it in a vacant spot in the living room. It looked peaceful enough, but I concluded that a bit of caution was recommended with those birds and all that water. I hoped the swans and geese would behave themselves and not start any arguments since it was a little crowded in that pool as well as the living room (a potential battlefield). I didn't think my house (or me) could take any more confrontations among those birds.

After leaving the peaceful swans alone in their pool, I checked the back porch to see if any peace existed back there. That was wishful thinking with those crazy geese running loose. I decided that all the other birds abiding there would have to sleep without covers on their cages. There was *no way* I was going to venture onto the back porch without a "battle plan" (or weapons) against those geese. It was just too dangerous!

I decided I would cover all the other cages inside my house (living room, dining room, kitchen, and den) and sit down for a few minutes to contemplate the situation. I couldn't believe how much this "bird sanctuary" had expanded inside my house. It had now swelled to four rooms. I should call it a zoo and charge admission.

<->

Just as I plopped my "expanding" posterior onto the couch I felt a sudden squish. Another goose egg! I needed to be more careful when I maneuvered around the house now, walking *and* sitting. Those geese were now attacking me and various parts of my anatomy in many diverse ways.

I covered the bird cages and decided to retire from the "battlefield" for the night. I started upstairs to bed with the satisfaction of having accidentally stepped into the swans' pool only three times. One of those steps, however, had occurred while I was chasing after a thirsty goose, which had promptly disappeared into another room. I had decided to change my strategy with these geese—to go on the offensive instead of the defensive. Unfortunately, I'd have to find them first, which was a potentially arduous and dangerous task!

I grabbed a broom, and with my "weapon in hand," I cautiously climbed the stairs toward my bedroom, keeping a close watch for any enemies I might encounter on the way. My house had become a "war zone."

I safely entered my bedroom, carefully looked around, checked all the closets, corners, and other possible hiding places that might harbor one of those dreaded geese, and finally determined that I was safe. Then, feeling secure with my broom close at hand, I finally relaxed, locked the door, and retired for the night.

The Eighth Day

I awoke early, cleaned up, and carefully made my way downstairs with my trusty broom. Fortunately, there were no goose attacks. Maybe they had all decided to sleep late. More than likely, they were probably all together somewhere, planning their "attack missions" for the day. I wondered if their battle cry was, "First this farmhouse and that crazy broom-lady, then the neighborhood!"

I had hoped that this day might bring an end to this fiasco of boxes and birds, but I should have known better. Unfortunately, arriving right on schedule were the same boxes and the same number of creatures. The pet shop must have gotten a new shipment of birds early that morning just for me. I also felt that some of the local farms might be supplying the geese that were being shipped to me. After all, what pet shop owner would want to keep a bunch of geese for sale in their shop? That would be too dangerous for everyone—the owner *and* the customers.

<->

The only bright spot of the day was the arrival of the

five gold rings. I had decided that the man who brought those gold rings must be associated with a local jewelry store. His demeanor certainly exhibited his knowledge of jewelry and the cautiousness of its delivery.

I had cashed in two rings the day before and used a small portion of the money to buy food for this bunch of flying, creeping, egg-laying, and swimming fowls. I was shocked at the resale value those rings provided. I should now have enough cash for months, safely locked away in my new safe.

<->

When I arrived at work, my boss told me it would be all right if I wanted to take a few days off while I resolved the "problem" I was having at my house. Well, that's what he told me, anyway. I think the birds' smell was following me to work.

I also observed a couple of my co-workers wrinkling up their noses when I walked by them. I wondered if they knew what it was like to live with a bunch of birds. I would certainly be delighted to lock them in my house for a couple of hours so they could find out!

With all the trouble I was having at home, I agreed with my boss about the time off. I did have some vacation time available, so I figured that should work out quite nicely.

After I returned home, I gave up trying to catch the geese that were still loose in the house. There were just too many hiding places, and they were too quick for me anyway. They were also too dangerous, especially with all their "search and destroy" missions against me.

I estimated that this "geese army" now had at least

twelve members, with six of them located on the back porch. This meant that six were still loose somewhere in the house. That was six geese to only one of me (plus one broom). Those still were not very good odds since my broom was only a "single shot" type—one swing at a time, with an effective range of only three or four feet— much too close for comfort!

I wasn't sure, but I thought one of the goose eggs had hatched. Recently, I was sure I heard a "peeping" noise from somewhere within the house. I figured the mother goose was hiding it from me for fear of retaliation! *Retaliation*? Why would I want to retaliate? I only wanted to *cook* a goose!

Much to my relief, an eighth box of new birds did NOT arrive this morning. All the others *did*, however. I decided to move those new boxes to the back porch, where all the other "foul" occupants were residing, or rather, had taken over.

Unfortunately, while I was carrying these boxes to the back porch, as I pulled open the back door, the six members of the "geese army" that were occupying that area all escaped (running right over me) through the open door and into the house.

Picking myself up off the floor, I shook my head angrily and watched the last goose disappear around a corner. Well, that did it. Now all 12 members of their army were loose in the place, and it looked like "war" had been declared. Unfortunately, no "peace negotiations" were being offered.

I left the new box of geese closed while I opened all the other new boxes. As usual, I found another partridge and tree, two more doves, three foreign chickens, four more calling birds, and seven more swans in their large pool (which I moved into the living room since it looked quite nice there).

My back porch was filled with cages of birds, and there was hardly any room to walk around. With some difficulty, I managed to feed all the regular birds and the new arrivals, which I had stuffed into the cages with their other existing relatives. Then, with much fear and trembling, I prepared myself for the next challenge.

I took a deep breath and looked at the unopened box of geese, which was all that remained to be completed for the day's deliveries. Hopefully, that would not be all that remained of my life. I detected all the nearby birds gasping for breath as I started for that final box. It had become very quiet on the porch, and all the birds were watching intently and waiting for the action to occur. I wondered if any bets were being taken as to the outcome of this dangerous mission and *who* they were betting on.

This time I left the door to the house unlocked for a quick getaway from the new boxed set of geese. I also had a small chair with me for protection. I figured that piece of furniture would help to hold off the nasty beasts while I slipped through the door and out of harm's way. I was beginning to feel like a lion tamer in a circus, minus a whip. Maybe I could use a whip next time if I lived long enough to locate one. Perhaps a shotgun would be better—nah, too noisy.

Well, I figured I'd stalled long enough and might as well get this fierce encounter over with. After loosening the top of the box, I didn't bother to dump the box over. Those six wild, hyperactive geese inside the box dumped it over for me. They only managed to rip off two chair legs before I escaped into the house, slamming the door behind me.

Now there were six more recruits into the "geese army" on the back porch and six—no, now twelve members (including at least two babies)—loose in the house somewhere. I felt like the odds of my survival were mounting against me.

Relieved after my escape (near-death experience) from those geese, I relaxed for a moment and glanced out the back window. It was then I noticed a small fenced pen next to the barn. I realized I hadn't seen that before.

Hmmm. These old farmhouses used to have some animals around, including geese. Maybe I could relocate my geese from the house to that pen. No, that would be like committing suicide with those nasty birds. Besides, I couldn't even find them, let alone capture and move them. I didn't even want to get near them.

On the other hand, that still might be a solution to the problem. That would take some more thought, though. Unfortunately, I would probably need a suit of armor if I was going to try anything that drastic.

<->

Later that afternoon, I totaled up the number of birds I'd received. That "birdbrained idiot"—who used to be my True Love—had sent me 92 birds! Why? I didn't know. My house had become an asylum for birds. A "funny farm" was a better description—with me as the chief "clown."

That birdbrain had also disconnected his phone and moved to parts unknown. His company didn't even know where he was, and neither did I. But his "calling cards" were all over my house!

<->

Well, late that afternoon, it finally happened. I heard a strange noise coming from behind the house. When I looked outside, I saw the source of that peculiar sound, which turned out to be my *newest* gift for the day.

A guy with a large cattle truck had just finished unloading his "delivery" and was knocking on the back door of my house. Fortunately, he hadn't gone to the back porch door, or he might have been assaulted and nearly killed by those crazy geese. Even though that door was closed, I'm sure those monsters would have found a way to open it. To those geese, the cattle truck driver was just another victim available to attack.

When I answered the door, he presented me with a receipt. Deciding that I had no choice in the matter, I signed it. He pointed toward the cattle and some ladies in my backyard and said, "They're all yours, now, lady. Enjoy them." He thanked me, got back into his truck, and pulled out of my driveway.

When I turned and looked in the backyard, I saw eight cows, accompanied by eight women dressed as milking maids. Of all the crazy gifts, this had to be the craziest one that this nut had come up with yet! Eight cows and eight milkmaids. Well, at least I might be able to sell the milk.

Since the backyard was extra large and thoroughly fenced in, there wouldn't be a problem with the cattle getting loose and wandering around the neighborhood. I think my backyard had just become a pasture. I guess you could say it was pasteurized!

As I watched, I noticed that those milking maids were very experienced in their work and had thoroughly mastered their routine. Since this looked like part of their regular job, I thought they probably had a contract with my *former* True Love.

Each one would milk a cow, then take the bucket of milk and dump it into a centralized container. I guess it was up to me to take care of the milk from that point on since it appeared that their job was then finished. A while later, a large van arrived, loaded up all the milkmaids, and sped away. The cows, however, remained. It didn't look like the cattle truck was going to return and pick them up.

Well, there I was, stuck with a large container of fresh raw milk left in the backyard. What do I do now? Well, there was nothing more I could do but talk to the experts. I called a few dairy farms in the area and asked for their advice about the problem.

The farmers I was able to talk with suggested that I contact a large, local dairy company to see if they would take the milk off my hands. I also noticed a few chuckles during my conversations with those farmers. They must have heard about my "plight" with my True Love guy and his gifts. They had probably even sold the cows to the guy!

Fortunately, the milk company I contacted agreed to buy the milk, beginning immediately. At least the milk wouldn't spoil overnight. They said they would return the next day and every day after as long as I needed them. What a break!

Since the cows were content to wander around and finally settle down for the night, I figured they would be okay until the morning. I also decided to check if the barn out back would be satisfactory enough to hold them during the night, if necessary. I wondered how long I was going to be stuck with them. I guess that was my decision since these were supposed to be gifts.

<->

I went through my nightly routine of covering bird cages, dodging "planted" goose eggs, and trying to keep from stepping in the swans' pools. My foot managed to find only three eggs and I only stepped in the swans' pools twice. I was improving and getting used to the "battlefield."

I decided to leave the back porch occupants as they were, seeing as how the geese were on the loose back there. It was suicidal to venture into that area! The other birds would just have to contend with the situation. Fortunately, I had already fed them earlier and had no reason to go back there.

I opened a few windows to air out the house and secretly hoped some of the geese might try to escape. After the way they handled my chair legs, I figured they wouldn't have any trouble escaping through windows.

After locking up the house for the night, I grabbed a book and my trusty broom and went upstairs to my bedroom. I checked for any enemies (geese) lurking about, then locked myself in. I read a book for a while in my room (it was too dangerous to read downstairs anymore), then went to bed.

The Ninth Day

The milking maids returned early this morning. The cows had been content to sleep and roam around the fenced backyard during the night. As long as they were comfortable, I decided to leave them there and not try to move them into the barn. Unfortunately, their "mooing" this morning had awakened me and some of my neighbors, who mentioned it to me in no uncertain terms. Maybe they would rather have a rooster wake them up. I'm sure that could be arranged!

I figured they were all city folks and were just not used to farm life. With all these animals around, I wasn't particularly fond of it either. I guess roosters were about the only birds missing in this madhouse.

As I looked out the window, I saw that the milkmaids were already hard at work, filling their buckets and then transferring the milk into the central container in the backyard. Fortunately, when the ladies had finished their job for the day, I only needed to call the milk company, and they would send a truck to pick up the milk and pay me for it. That was a relief—and profitable too, seeing as how the milkmaids and cows didn't cost me anything.

<->

The box of gold rings came early, as usual, with a smile and a wink from the deliveryman. "Hmmm, he is kind of cute," I told the birds. "And, he does seem like a rather nice, sympathetic man. He's rather curious, too." I made a mental note to formally introduce myself next time. I also decided to quit talking to that bunch of birds.

In the meantime, eight more cows arrived, along with their milking maids. That's *16* of each, now. By spring, I think I'll probably have the greenest backyard in the neighborhood. Unfortunately, I'm afraid it may also be the smelliest!

I'm thankful that there was lots of room for the cows and milkmaids, and they weren't stepping on each other. I'm also glad a milk company was coming to pick up the milk. This set of gifts sure was turning out to be a profitable venture, and I was finally seeing a return on my "non-investment."

<->

Back on the "home front," the usual boxes arrived right on schedule. This time, I had the pet store deliveryman open all the boxes inside the back porch and turn the birds loose. I also figured he could handle the geese better than I could. It was getting too dangerous to venture inside the porch now anyway. Fortunately, after he had released the geese, he was able to escape with only a torn coat sleeve. He was certainly a lot quicker than I at releasing them and getting away. It's also possible that fearing for his life may have had something to do with it.

I was having little trouble feeding and caring for the birds now. I was even able to clean up all their messes and tolerate all the overpowering odors without gagging! I guess I was getting used to them or something. That was a little worrisome.

At least that "idiot" (my former True Love) didn't send any *new* types of birds that day. I think *115* birds of any type is enough! I just received the usual count of the original species of birds. The *usual count?* The *original species* of birds? It was becoming *too* routine now.

<->

Later in the day, when I was finally getting some rest, the doorbell rang. I cautiously opened the door, and in walked some ladies—*nine* to be exact—all dressed in some rather "flimsy" costumes. One of these flimsy-costumed females smiled, said "hello," and handed me a card announcing that these nine overexposed "babes," err, ladies, were my new gifts for the day. One of them was carrying some sort of music player, which she set down on a table. When she turned it on, some strange music began to play.

I watched with interest and amusement as these ladies in their flimsy costumes, tried to dance around my living room. Fortunately, there was still a small bit of area left, despite all the assorted birds and trees. Some of their dances (and costumes) were a little questionable, leading me to conclude that I didn't want any children or men around watching them.

A few of those dancers wrinkled up their noses at the strange smells, but I knew they'd get used to it if they were going to be around for very long. Since these ladies were my new gifts for the day, I guessed the birds and I would have to put up with them—and us with them! At least the cows weren't dancing around! That would make it extremely difficult for the milking maids and no doubt produce some instant milkshakes.

<->

Later in the day, after the daily milk pickup, I looked out the back window again and focused on the fenced-in pen next to the barn, which I figured was probably an old pig pen. I had now decided that I would dump the new shipment of geese in there tomorrow. I didn't even question whether a new shipment would arrive since I knew it would.

Whether it was an old pig pen or not, I figured it should work out just fine as a "geese pen" since I didn't think there was much difference between pigs and those geese anyway.

<->

Toward the end of the afternoon, after all the new human guests (dancing ladies) left for their probable night jobs, I made sure that all the birds found accommodations for the night throughout my house.

I had also given up trying to keep all the birds located in certain areas, as well as in their cages. Most of them now had complete freedom of the house—chiefly because I couldn't find or catch all of them. Those birds that I could catch, I stuffed into the appropriate cages for the night. The others were on their own. I hoped that they would all get along and that no disagreements or fights would break out during the night. I also hoped that some of them might find their way out through an open window!

I found out later that some of them (doves and calling birds) *had* ventured out through the open windows. I certainly wasn't going to lose any sleep over that. They could survive in the "wild" and get all the food or bird seed they needed from my outside bird feeder, which I kept filled most of the time.

<->

Satisfied that everything was in order, I locked up the house and started to retreat to my upstairs bedroom. I grabbed a weapon (my trusty broom), and after going through my routine of carefully checking for any lurking terrorists (geese), I started up the stairs.

As I neared the top of the stairs, a sudden movement in the shadows off to my left caught my attention, and I stopped to check it out, wondering why I was doing such a dangerous thing. The prudent thing to do was to ignore it and run! I guess I was too scared to even do that.

I noticed the disturbance was coming from one of the spare bedrooms. I eased back away from the open door to that room and saw that my hands were shaking a bit. Yeah, my hands were only shaking slightly, but I think my shivering body was causing the whole house to shake!

Well, I had gone this far, so I thought I might as well go ahead and check out the darkened room. Visions of a drooling five-foot, 200-pound monster goose or a hideous extraterrestrial alien waiting to pounce on me crept into my thoughts while I brought my now puny-looking broom up to an *attack* position.

I wondered why I was doing such a stupid thing as I slowly peeked around the door into that dark room. Suddenly, I felt cold air blowing on my face and heard a flapping noise coming from inside the room. I was sure it was the cold breath coming from some six-foot, 300-pound gigantic goose loose in the room.

I also thought I detected a kind of scratching sound emanating from the room. I had convinced myself that the sound belonged to a seven-foot, 350-pound goose that was sharpening his beak on the floor of the room, just waiting for me to enter!

Nevertheless, I was determined to see this through, even though I was convinced this goose had to be at least nine feet tall and weigh 450 pounds. I raised my broom again and jumped through the open door while yelling like a karate novice—all sound and no action! I swung my broom around a few times and succeeded in hitting nothing but lots of cold air.

When I finally stopped and regained my senses, I reached over to the wall and switched on the light—what I should have done in the first place instead of acting like an idiot! I guess I needed the exercise anyway.

As I looked around the room, I immediately saw what the mysterious movement was. It was only an open window, which was allowing cold air to blow into the room and making the curtains move, therefore creating that flapping noise I'd heard. As I felt that breeze flowing into the room, it was no wonder I froze in place. That air was cold! I also saw a couple of tree limbs scraping against the window, which was the scratching sound I had heard.

Breathing a sigh of relief, I quickly walked across the room, reached up, lowered the window, and locked it, cutting off the freezing outside air. I chuckled a little, thinking what a great video clip that would make. I wondered how many views it would get. The title would probably be, "Ten-foot, 500-pound monster goose vanishes into cold, thin air with one swish of the broom!" I laughed out loud and turned around, switched out the light, and headed for my room.

I finally reached my room safely, entered it, checked for any rogue geese, and locked the door. After I had stopped shaking, I sat down, relaxed a little, and read a humorous book for a while with my broom next to me. I certainly didn't want to read a thriller after all I'd just been through.

<->

Later on, I heard some strange noises coming from the downstairs kitchen and figured that the geese were just helping themselves to any food they could procure, or steal. That was fine with me as long as I didn't have to confront (or feed) any of them. They had already taken most of my house captive, so why not the kitchen also?

As things finally quieted down around the house (loony bin), I crawled into bed and drifted off to sleep, wondering what gifts would arrive the next day.

The Tenth Day

I finally decided to use the old pig pen beside the barn in the backyard to house the new horde of geese that would probably arrive this morning (I didn't even question their arrival anymore). I figured if that pen could hold a bunch of pigs, it could undoubtedly handle those geese. From what I had seen, I didn't think there was too much difference between the two.

The fence around the pen looked tall and strong enough so that the geese couldn't escape and threaten the whole neighborhood with a siege. There was also a connecting door from the pen into the barn, and a separate fenced area inside that could accommodate (incarcerate) the geese. That would prevent them from roaming around and destroying the entire barn.

I figured when I closed up for the night, I could open the door to the barn and chase them inside, where they could spend the night in a warm and safe place. Mostly, safe for me (and the neighborhood).

<->

I delightedly received my daily shipment of rings from the "gold ring" deliveryman, thanked him, and prepared myself for the rest of the day. He was getting friendlier every day. He was certainly more interesting than that bunch of birds.

When the pet store deliveryman arrived with the usual assortment of birds, I had him put all the other boxes of birds on the back porch, except for the geese. I told him about my plan to utilize the old pig pen beside the barn. He thought it was a good idea that might just work. I may have influenced his decision when I told him that *he* would be occupying the pen with the geese if he didn't help me with the plan.

He lugged the box of geese out to the pen and set it down. He turned and quickly started walking toward his truck without opening the box. He was getting as difficult to handle as the geese. After catching and dragging him back from his truck, I forced him to open and dump the box of geese into the pen beside the barn. This idea worked quite well, and the geese only stole his hat during the process.

He went off shaking and mumbling some nasty comments about the geese. He also muttered something about me, but I couldn't quite hear it. He backed out of my driveway and "laid rubber" (put the pedal to the metal) down the street. What a big showoff—all because he lost his hat! I was sure the pet shop would buy him another one.

<->

Later, after I had unpacked the usual deliveries of assorted birds and trees, the rest of the gifts (cows, milkmaids, and lady dancers) arrived for the day, along with a new *human* group. There were ten of them in the new bunch. They were all male dancers (much to the delight of the lady dancers), with an obsession for jumping and leaping around while they danced. In my very crowded living room, this had all the potential for a few broken ceiling lights, not to mention some broken heads. Well, at least I knew that my *once* True Love was still active in his "gift department" toward me.

<-->

Just about all the *138* birds (I can't believe I can say that number so calmly) that I had received were loose now, singing, chirping, screeching, swimming, fighting, flying, creeping, and leaving their "decorations" all over the house and back porch.

While trying to ignore all the different noises and other "extracurricular" activities among the dancers, I decided to take inventory again. What else was there to do?

I knew I had **27** gold rings left, but I didn't know how many more to expect. I decided to hold on to as many of them as possible, hoping that gold prices would increase again. Some of those were safe and secure in a bank's safe deposit box. I kept the others at home in my new safe as "petty cash" for necessities.

I also had **10** pear trees, **10** partridges, **18** doves, **24** French (soon to be *fried*) chickens, **28** birds calling to each other (for whatever reason), **30** of those wretched geese—minus the **6** in the barn pen—not to mention several eggs and babies, and **28** swans quietly occupying four small pools of water.

Out in the backyard, I counted **24** cows and **24** milking maids. I noticed that the cows' smell (fertilizer) was getting rather strong and decided I'd better call some local farmers (before the neighbors called me) to see if they might take some of it off my hands—or, rather, the backyard pasture.

In the living room, there were now **18** lady dancers trying to dance, or whatever, who were also eyeing some of the male dancers, while some of the **10** male dancers were trying to dance with the ladies. It sure hadn't taken very long for each group to give up their individual dancing assignments and "combine forces."

In addition, there were a few faces slapped (both male and female), along with some further exclamations of pain from someone stepping—or stomping—on the toes of another dancer (male and female). This was primarily due to the increasingly congested conditions in the living room. Otherwise, the dancers were just plain clumsy (male and female). The whole situation was beginning to look more "explosive" all the time, which was *definitely* an understatement!

<->

Toward evening, after I had put up with this racket all day, I dismissed (kicked out) all the human guests to let them retire to their various lodgings and night jobs. The lady milkmaids had already left and returned to their different farms to check out for the day, leaving the cows content (fat, dumb, and happy) in the backyard.

I grabbed my trusty broom and walked out through the backyard cow pasture to the barn pen, carefully watching where I stepped. I carefully maneuvered to the side of the barn where the door was, quickly reached over the pen's fence, unlatched, and pushed open the door to the barn. Fortunately, the latch on the door was high enough to prevent the geese from reaching it—and me.

Moving back to the front of the pen, I reached over the fence and started swinging my broom back and forth among the geese. I forced them into the barn, and then, grabbing a rope I had attached to the barn door, I pulled it shut and latched it. Well, that worked better than I thought it would. After that confrontation with the geese, I still had half my broom left. Satisfied that one of my ideas had finally worked, I turned and carefully made my way back to the house.

I breathed a sigh of relief, then remembered I had to open some windows before I went upstairs. By opening a few windows to eliminate some of the obnoxious odors, I also hoped that some of the more adventurous birds might decide to explore the open windows as well as the great outdoors.

I noticed that the birds' smell was getting a bit ripe again. It also occurred to me to check my shoes to make sure *I* wasn't contributing to the in-house odors due to my excursion in the back pasture. Fortunately, I hadn't tracked in any additional unwanted aromas.

<->

I fed the birds, locked up for the night, and with my "half" broom weapon in hand, raced up the stairs to my room before I could be attacked by any outlaw creatures. I thought I'd better buy a new broom tomorrow for better protection. No, I'd better make it two brooms— one as reserve ammunition.

I slammed my bedroom door shut and immediately

found a goose egg under my foot! Aaagh! That was enough! I was about to declare war again on a bunch of geese and their "land mines"!

I contemplated returning to the kitchen to sharpen my knives in anticipation of "inviting" a goose to Sunday dinner. However, I decided it was much too dangerous to venture out of my bedroom onto the dark stairs with those marauding beasts running around loose. I also didn't think I could gain access to the hall light switch before one of them could gain access to me!

I knew I was much safer in my room and was in no mood for a "search-and-destroy" mission that night—especially with a defective weapon (half a broom). I decided to plan my strategy for the next day and then retire for the night.

The Eleventh Day

All the human participants returned, and the other usual deliveries arrived early that day (I couldn't believe how routine this had become). In addition, the dancing ladies increased their number by nine today. The **27** female dancers were now bumping into and falling all over each other as they desperately tried to dance and eye all the men in the room simultaneously.

The number of male dancers had increased to **20**, all trying to dance and eye the lady dancers. And, oh yes, a new male group had arrived—a bunch of "pipers" or flute players. There were **11** flutists, pipers, or whatever they're called, all playing somewhat the same tune, or so it seemed.

All the dancers had now discarded their original music in favor of the pipers' tunes. I also noticed that some of the pipers had discarded their flutes in favor of some of the lady dancers. With the male dancers displaying somewhat the same inclination toward the lady dancers, something told me this was going to get out of hand rather quickly!

WHAT A RACKET! My living room, dining room, den, and other rooms had become a madhouse! There were 58 people playing flutes or dancing and leaping all over the place (or trying to). Birds were flying around and occasionally dropping "bombs" on the humans below, and the geese were running around attacking anything that moved, as well as depositing eggs and other natural material around the house. It all looked and sounded like a terrible nightmare—not to mention how it smelled!

As I glanced around, I observed that most of the goose eggs were immediately being smashed, scrambled, and squashed by the dancing people because of the continual action taking place in the house. I also noticed that the male "admirers" of the lady dancers were tossing a few eggs at each other as the competition for the lady dancers' affections had become more violent. Man, was this ever going to get interesting!

I determined that any of those eggs not meeting that "crushing" fate would be cooked and served for my breakfast the following day. I was also still planning a dinner for the geese, with some of them becoming the main dish!

I spent a lot of my time trying to gather up those precious and free "food items" (eggs) without getting kicked and knocked out in the process! After a while, I got pretty good at dodging all the moving bodies and flying feet. The flute players were getting pretty good at playing their flutes while they danced (or whatever) with the ladies. Unfortunately, their music suffered quite a bit from attempting to play and dance at the same time.

The shaky, off-key music was especially evident when another male participant—also competing for the dancing ladies' affections—expressed his dissatisfaction to the flute player with a swift kick in the pants. An explanation for this assumed "indiscretion" by the male dancer (he had just slipped on the carpet) was sometimes answered by a rather vigorous push or bump from the flute player, resulting in a further confrontation between the two of them on the floor.

Sometimes this angry encounter would result in the two "wrestlers" accidentally tripping one or two of the dancing ladies, who then became involuntarily involved in the fracas by falling into the mess. The entire free-for-all was usually brought to an abrupt end by someone (me) grabbing a bucket of water from the swans' pool and pouring it on them. That "peace negotiation" seemed to subdue everyone until the next "showdown" occurred.

There was also a moment when one of the male dancers accidentally mistook me for a dancing lady. He was an excellent dancer, and we both enjoyed it. I felt very honored, even though he apologized profusely for his mistake—with a very nice smile. Imagine that. I was mistaken for a dancing lady—and without a flimsy costume too! Oh well, he probably needed glasses anyway.

<->

Earlier, the pet store deliveryman had deposited (dumped) the latest box of geese into the barn pen. This time he left his hat in his truck, so the geese had nothing to steal from him. After his deliveries, he departed (slower this time), and everything seemed to return to normal. Normal? How could this madhouse be normal?

In the backyard, the cows and milking maids were scattered all over the place, each doing their jobs efficiently. The grass was already getting greener; the milk company was now picking up milk three times a day, and the cows' smell wasn't getting any worse. I was also able to contact a farmer who agreed to stop by and pick up the cow "fertilizer." That would certainly help alleviate the backyard aroma. All this had become quite an efficient operation—as well as a profitable one, too.

I noticed that some of the flute players had now abandoned my living room for the backyard—and the milkmaids. I thought they might have had a financial interest in my backyard business, but these guys seemed to be more interested in the human aspect of the backyard than the efficient milk operation. I decided these flute guys were not interested in dairy farming but more in visiting with the employees of the dairy operation.

<->

Financially, I sold some of the gold rings, which had increased in value again, and purchased a rather large Individual Retirement Account. The pet store and some of the local farms had finally offered to buy some (but not all) of those filthy birds from me—at a wholesale price, of course. That would ease the space problem in my house by quite a bit. No doubt the birds had been purchased from these people—at a much higher price. I think somebody was making a lot of money from all this.

<->

I wondered if I would ever see my ex-True Love again, who had been so generous in sending me all these gifts. I had other items available that would produce some "goose eggs" on him if he ever showed up. A toss into the geese pen out back would be a good start!

Finally, after all the humans left for the day, I went out to the barn in the backyard, sneaked in through the barn's front door, and closed the outside pen door where all the geese were.

While the geese were busy wondering why they had been isolated in the outside pen, I filled a couple of large watering dishes and dumped some grain into them. I had read that geese wouldn't choke to death if they ate the grain when it was wet. Although it was a difficult decision to make, I figured I'd better feed them the correct way and keep those creatures alive if I was going to realize any revenue from them. I wasn't worried about feeding the ones in the house since they were stealing food from my kitchen every night.

I hurriedly finished the feeding preparations and decided to get out of the barn before those hyperactive geese battered down the door. From the violent uproar they were causing, it sounded like they had obtained a battering ram and were using it against the door. They must have realized that I was inside! I didn't have a chair, broom, or a spare deliveryman with me, so I quickly opened the outside door to the pen, leaped (crawled) over the inside fence, and hurried out the front door of the barn, locking it behind me.

Fortunately, those geese were so intent on battering down that side door that they never saw me leave. They rushed into the barn and went straight for the water dishes containing the food. While they were busily competing among themselves for the food, I rushed around the side of the barn to the pen, reached over the fence, and pulled the pen door closed. They were now locked in the barn for the night, and I was safe—at least for this night.

After I returned to the house, I fed the other birds and locked up the house. I did remember to open a few windows since a fresh breeze throughout the house was *desperately* needed. Again, I just couldn't believe how routine all that had become.

<->

I went into the kitchen, grabbed my "half" broom (the one the geese had torn up), and started upstairs for my room with my weapon in hand. I had decided to "arm" myself on my trek upstairs to the bedroom. This time, if *anything* moved, so would my broom!

Fortunately, I successfully maneuvered my way through the battlefield area and entered my bedroom without encountering any enemy geese.

Once inside, I checked the room for any hidden opposition but found none. I then closed and locked the door.

A few minutes later, I heard noises in the downstairs kitchen. The geese were raiding the kitchen again, stealing all the food I had left out for them. I didn't mind, as long as I didn't have to risk my life trying to feed them.

With my trusty "half" broom beside me, I began to relax and settled down with a good book. I wondered when this siege would end. It needed to be soon because I was close to running out of weapons (brooms, chairs, and deliverymen).

The Twelfth Day

Though I didn't know it yet, this was the last day I would receive any of these crazy gifts. I already had enough gifts and, unfortunately, didn't know how to return some of these "favors" to the individual who was no longer my True Love.

<->

Early this morning, I was suddenly shocked out of my sleep, as well as my bed, by the sound of drums—lots of drums! Picking myself up off the floor, I unlocked and opened my bedroom door, rushed out of the room, and started down the stairs. I suddenly stopped, reversed course, and hurried back into my bedroom. I then reappeared wearing my nightgown (all this nonsense was making me forgetful) and rushed down the stairs to the living room to see what was going on!

Looking out the window, I soon discovered the source of the disturbance. There in my front yard were *12* uniformed individuals marching around with drums and drumsticks, loudly displaying their noisy abilities.

I also noticed that some of the neighbors were out on their porches, displaying their dissatisfaction while checking out the noisy individuals on my front lawn. Most of them just shook their heads, while a few shook their fists in my direction, and then retreated into their houses.

The other human "gifts" were already on the front lawn, talking with each other and drinking coffee. They were all lined up and waiting to get in. I figured if any neighbors had decided to hang around for that day, they would certainly leave now.

I noticed that the flute players had added *11* more to their ranks, and...oh, never mind. Just let me list the final inventory since *no more* of these insane gifts arrived after this day. HOORAY!

At the last count, my stupid, insane ex-friend (True love) had sent me the following items—and skipped town!

12 Pear trees - All these were suitable for planting in the spring. I decided that I could also use the decorative wooden pots in which these trees had been shipped. I calculated that most of those would bring a reasonable price at a garage sale.

12 Partridges - Some of these birds had started fighting with the geese (when they came out of hiding) just to relieve the boredom. It was kind of a repeat of David and Goliath, with Goliath prevailing this time.

22 Turtledoves – A few of these "peaceful" birds were now fighting with each other. They probably got tired of hearing all that never-ending "cooing."

30 French hens - When these foreign chickens weren't fighting with the other birds—which was like World War II all over again—they were looking for French *roosters!*

36 **Calling birds** – If they weren't calling their bookies, they seemed to be doing nothing but making noise and leaving lots of their "calling cards."

40 **Gold rings** - Many of these were sold, and some of the money was used to buy food for those filthy birds. The rest of that money was used to purchase numerous money-making bank accounts. The other rings were kept in a bank's safe deposit box for any future investments. I also kept a couple of rings in my brand-new safe for petty cash.

42 **Miserable geese** - These "foul" fowls in the barn pen were still trying to beat down the pen door and the fence around the pen. The geese that were still in the house were running around acting like commandos. They were attacking from ambush, then running and hiding, waiting to strike again. In addition, they were laying eggs (squishy land mines) all over the place. Those eggs that hadn't hatched were just waiting for some unsuspecting, misplaced human foot (namely mine) to discover them!

42 **Swimming swans** - These peaceful waterfowl were quietly swimming around in six portable water pools located in the living and dining rooms. They seemed quite subdued, despite the rather overcrowded, noisy conditions and constant tussles and intrusions from the dancing humans who kept stepping into their swimming pools. Some of these peaceful waterfowl occasionally "lost their cool" at the invasive humans by nipping at a few feet!

40 Dairy cows – These wonderful animals were diligently producing milk daily and, with the help of the milkmaids, were adding very nicely to my income. They were also freely fertilizing my back pasture, thus making it the greenest area in the neighborhood. In addition, I was also selling most of their "fertilizer" to a local farmer who was picking it up daily. So far, the neighbors (those still around) hadn't complained about the noise or the smell. They must have had worn-out hearing aids and bad sinus conditions!

40 Milking maids - These hard-working ladies were responsible for milking the cows and providing the particular substance (milk) that added to my daily income. I also happened to notice that a few of the more energetic ladies occasionally took some time away from their responsibilities to chase after the dancing men and flute players. The rest of the ladies just waited for those guys to find *them*.

36 Dancing ladies - Those ladies, in their "flimsy" costumes, were all trying to dance around my living room and dining room, despite the overcrowded conditions. In this situation, they certainly didn't look like graceful swans.

Those who didn't pursue any of the dancing men or flute players suffered numerous bumps, bruises, sore toes, and other bruised parts of their anatomy as they faithfully tried to dance (and fall) in such a confined area.

Some of them had just given up and were sitting down, relaxing, and drinking the coffee I had provided. They were also exchanging a few "political" views with the dancing men and flute players, who seemed to be more interested in exchanging *other* views with these lady dancers.

30 Dancing, or Leaping men - These guys had tried their best to dance and leap but had only succeeded in bumping, bruising, tripping, falling, and banging into one another in the living room and dining room. Because of the increasingly fierce competition between these guys for the milkmaids and dancing ladies, some of the brawling, bumping, bruising, and banging had become increasingly deliberate and rather violent.

22 Flute players or Pipers - I'm certainly glad these musicians weren't playing tubas. Now, if they were only able to play the same tune at the same time...oh, well. Most of these players who were able to find a small area in the living room (about two square feet), played their instruments as best they could. The others were just playing with the dancing ladies and milkmaids.

12 **Drum players with drums** - Where it was possible, these uniformed marchers occupied positions in the living room. However, being latecomers to this insane "gathering," they hadn't had much orientation time or training on how to properly handle themselves with the situation involving all the other human occupants inside and outside the house. But they learned fast and entered the fierce "competition" for the dancers and milkmaids with drumsticks *swinging*! Also, in addition to banging on their drums, they were skillfully pounding their drumsticks on the heads of birds and anything else that irritated them—human or otherwise.

Fortunately, by the end of the day, these characters and creatures were no longer in my presence. I had negotiated with the milk company and some farmers to remove (unload) all the cows (plus fertilizer) and the milkmaids (no offense to them). Furthermore, all the birds were gone. Some had flown out the windows, and others had been sent to local farms, pet shops, and various dining room tables. Someone even bought all those miserable geese—at a discount, of course. I didn't care, since I was delighted to get rid of all those critters and receive something in return from the sales.

****

Well, there you have it, the story of my "Twelve days and nightmares" after Christmas. What a ZOO! I don't think I ever want to see another bird again, especially in my house! I'm not particularly enthusiastic about dancers or musicians, either.

Anyway, after more than 12 days and nights of this craziness, I'd had enough and decided to take action. After locating all the human gifts (dancers, flutists, and drummers) from around the house and other areas, I gathered them all together, thanked them for their efforts, and told them in a "polite" way to GET OUT! As far as I was concerned, their contract with my former "friend" was terminated, much to their pleasure as well. They were more than happy to leave and get away from this crazy place too. I'm sure some of them also had some newfound relationships they wanted to pursue.

Epilogue

It has now been six months since all these screwball events occurred. Many things have transpired since then. Please allow me to bring you up to date.

After a great deal of cleanup, which included carpet replacement, I was able to return to a more sane, calm, and stable way of life again. Even the neighbors were communicating with me—in a friendly way this time.

When they finally heard the truth about all that had transpired, a number of them were rather sympathetic, and some even offered to help me with the cleanup. Unfortunately, I observed that most of them were suddenly quite busy with yardwork and other things and were rarely available for any assistance. Oh well, at least they were talking to me again.

<->

Since I was legally declared the owner of the cows and milkmaid employees because I had received each of them as gifts, I elected to remain in the dairy business as a silent partner with the milk company. The milk business proved to be successful for me, as well as very profitable. The dairy company was in favor of the idea because they could use the extra revenue as well as the cows and milking maids, who were both experienced in the more modern methods of milk production.

<->

Things also turned out very well for me, thanks to the gold rings. The investments I made by selling some of them proved very profitable. I also decided to have my journal printed, from which I recorded all these memorable (?) events. A publisher gave me a rather large and generous down payment for it. He thinks the journal could become a bestseller! Well, we'll wait and see about that.

In addition, those gold rings turned out to be worth a lot more than anyone thought they would. The price of gold changes rapidly. Fortunately, I was able to sell some of them when gold prices increased.

<->

But I still wonder how he, my ex-True Love (birdbrain, idiot, creep, or whatever), was able to purchase (or rip off) all those gold rings. I guess I just have an inquisitive mind. In addition, my suspicions were aroused when some detectives and FBI agents came around asking questions about him. I was successful in persuading them that he was simply a friend I knew and wasn't "in cahoots" with him regarding any stolen goods. Also, after hearing about all the "gifts" he had sent to me, they had no trouble believing my explanation.

As of this writing, they still haven't been able to locate him. Maybe they should check around the Carribean Islands.

Oh well, what's done is done—thankfully! It certainly was an experience that I wouldn't ever want to repeat—especially with those wretched geese!

<->

All in all, I think everything turned out all right. I am now part owner of a very profitable dairy business, and I'm also newly married. In case you hadn't heard, I married the gold ring delivery man. It turned out that he was the owner of a local jewelry store. Another very good investment!

Gift Inventory
(in order of delivery)

1 **Partridge in a Pear tree** (I hate pears.) – <u>total</u> = **12** (birds + trees)

2 **Turtledoves** ("cooing" all the time.) - <u>total</u> = **22** (birds)

3 **French Hens** (looking for fights and French roosters.) - <u>total</u> = **30** (birds)

4 **Calling Birds** (with "calling cards.") - <u>total</u> = **36** (birds)

5 **Gold Rings** (continually increasing in value.) - <u>total</u> = **40** ($$$$$)

6 **Geese a-Laying** (commandos in training.) - <u>total</u> = **42** (birds + eggs and babies)

7 **Swans a-Swimming** (all getting water logged.) - <u>total</u> = **42** (birds)

8 **Maids a-Milking** (milking the cows and being chased by the dancing men and pipers. Some of them were chasing the pipers.) - <u>total</u> = **40** (humans + cows)

9 **Ladies Dancing** (dancing and chasing the pipers and dancing men. Other ladies were being chased by *all* the men.) - <u>total</u> = **36** (humans + sore feet and other bruised parts of their anatomy.)

10 Lords a-Leaping (dancing men; dancing, jumping, leaping, falling, brawling, chasing the dancing ladies, and being chased by the ladies.) - <u>total</u> = **30** (humans + bruised bodies)

11 Pipers Piping (tooting their flutes while chasing the milkmaids and dancing ladies when not being chased by the milkmaids.) - <u>total</u> = **22** (humans + flutes)

12 Drummers Drumming (beating their drums and everything else in sight.) - <u>total</u> = **12** (humans + drums)

+ **3** bottles of **aspirin.**

Comments from Interested and Uninterested Observers

"I was wondering (sniff) what that strange odor was about her."

> — **Beulah "Big-nose" Buttercup** (a workmate of Bunny)

"I was a little suspicious about what was going on. There was something that just wasn't quite right about that girl. Something just didn't smell right."

> — **Percy Hicklebun, XIV** (Bunny's boss who sent her home for the week)

"She sure looked funny crawling through that window."

> — **Norma Buttinsky** (a neighbor's comment when Bunny was locked out of her house)

"*You* should talk! You couldn't even begin to crawl through a window!"

> — **Gus Buttinsky** (Norma's husband making a *very dangerous* remark)

"Gus, are you okay? Here, let me help you up. That Norma, she sure can throw a mean punch!"

> — **Otto D. Meddler** (Gus's neighbor, after seeing Norma's belt to Gus's jaw)

"I hate geese! I hate birds! I hate all these boxes! I hate pet shops! Where's my new hat?"

> — **Bubba D. Liverer** (Pet shop deliveryman after his last delivery to Bunny's house)

"Shore, little lady (ptooey!). Be glad ta' take the stuff off yer' hands, err, out of yer' field (ptooey!). Like a chaw a' tobacky?"

> — **Mel S. Badd** (a local farmer surveying the cow pasture situation; very handy with a shovel)

"I've enjoyed the work here. It's a very nice farmhouse. Say, which way did that flute player go?"

> — **Zelda Sweetlips** (a Milking maid commenting and *surveying* the situation while milking her cows)

"Honk, Honk!"

> — **Goose "Army" Leader** (from somewhere inside the house)

"OOF! (Thump!)"

> — **Bertha Bighips** (a Dancing lady encountering a wall— an unmovable object)

"Well, hello! Let me help you up."

> — **Lance "Twinkletoes" Bubblebrain** (a male dancer encountering a fallen dancing lady—an attractive movable object)

"Oh yuck!"

> — **Humphrey Horntweeter** (a Piping piper stepping on a goose egg while trying to dance and play his flute)

88

"Ouch! Get off my foot, you big buffalo!"
— **Thelma Coldfingers** (a Milking maid encountering a problem with her cow)

"(Wham!) Get away from me, you filthy goose!"
— **Wilberdorf Dumbswatty** (a drummer taking the offensive by using his drumstick against the head of a goose. A potentially *dangerous* action)

"$20 on 'Crawling Eagle' to win in the Sixth."
— **Unknown** (someone or something overheard making a call to his bookie)

"Hello. Welcome to *Pets Sure 'R' Your Friends*, the only store that will satisfy all your pet's needs (and my wallet). Now, how much would you like to spend...err, what kind of expensive pet can I interest you in?"
— **Oliver Dumcluck** (a Pet shop owner)

"Listen, big, tall, and stupid! Quit stomping on my feet!"
— **Lulu Chunkydumpling** (a lady dancer responding to a male dancer's clumsy attempt at trying to dance with her)

A Gift for You

Everyone likes to receive a gift, especially because it's free. The most important gift you can receive is eternal life through Jesus Christ. A verse in the Bible, John, chapter 3, verse 16 says, *"For God so loved the world, that he gave his only begotten Son, that whosoever believeth in him should not perish, but have everlasting life."* God will give the gift of salvation to anyone who will accept it. A gift is always freely given, but a person must choose to accept it, or he cannot have it.

The Bible teaches that because of our sins, we all fall short of the perfect righteousness required for us to be able to live with God in Heaven. He is holy and just, and no amount of good works will ever remove that debt of sin from us. *"For all have sinned, and come short of the glory of God" (Romans 3:23).* Baptism cannot save you from hell either.

Because we sin against the Holy God, we deserve punishment—death and separation from God in hell forever. *"For the wages of sin is death" (Romans 6:23).* But God has provided a way for us to be saved from this punishment, to have our sins forgiven, and to be able to go to Heaven. *"But God commendeth his love toward us, in that, while we were yet sinners, Christ died for us" (Romans 5:8).*

God's Son, Jesus Christ, suffered and died in our place on the cross of Calvary. He came to earth, lived a perfect, sinless life, and was the perfect substitute for us by taking upon Himself all our sins and the penalty of eternal death in Hell. *"Who his own self bare our sins in his own body on the tree, that we, being dead to sins, should live unto righteousness: by whose stripes ye were healed" (1 Peter 2:24).*

Salvation from hell is a gift God gives to us according to His grace, mercy, and love. Because salvation is a gift, you cannot earn it or buy it; you can only accept it from God. *"...but the gift of God is eternal life through Jesus Christ our Lord" (Romans 6:23b).*

You either accept Jesus Christ as your Savior or reject Him. It's a choice you alone must make. No one can make that decision for you. If you *accept* Him, you will receive the gift of eternal life in Heaven. If you *reject* Him by refusing His gift, you will pay the punishment for your sins by spending eternity in a never-ending burning hell. *"For by grace are ye saved through faith; and that not of yourselves: it is the gift of God: Not of works, lest any man should boast" (Ephesians 2:8, 9).*

Do not wait any longer to accept Jesus as your Savior. You may not live another day. Bow your head and talk to God right now. Ask Him to forgive your sins and to save you from hell. *"That if thou shalt confess with thy mouth the Lord Jesus, and shalt believe in thine heart that God hath raised him from the dead, thou shalt be saved. For with the heart man believeth unto righteousness; and with the mouth confession is made unto salvation" (Romans 10:9,10).*

" ...behold, now is the accepted time; behold, now is the day of salvation" (2 Corinthians 6:2b).

About the Author

Dick Foster is a retired computer professional who worked as a programmer and database analyst for over thirty years. Now, during his retirement, Dick likes to spend his time writing Biblical short stories for children and different types of humor. He lives in Greenville, SC.

Other Books By the Author

Children's Books

The Kids of Faith Learn Bible Truths

The Kids of Faith Learn More Bible Truths

Humor Books

"We Should Have Taken A Plane!"
Humorous Terms and Definitions of Family Travel by Automobile

Printed in Great Britain
by Amazon